The KnowHow Book of Puppets

Written and devised by
Violet Philpott and Mary Jean McNeil
Educational Adviser Sally Chaplin

Illustrated by Malcolm English
Designed by John Jamieson
Photographs by Brian Marshall

With the help of Deva Cook

First published in 1975
Usborne Publishing Ltd
20 Garrick Street
London WC2

© Usborne Publishing Ltd 1975

Printed in Great Britain by
Purnell & Sons Ltd
Bristol

About this Book

This is a book which tells you how to make lots of different kinds of puppets and how to work them properly when you have made them. You will find that the puppets at the beginning are easier to make than those at the end.

At the end of the book there are three puppet plays. We have started them, leaving you to make up the rest of the story yourself.

The puppets are made from things you will probably be able to find at home. A lot of them are made with glue. When you buy glue, remember to buy strong, quick drying glue like Bostik 1 and UHU. See page 46 for what glue to use on special materials.

Boxes with a sign like this show you how to do things which you may need to know on other pages as well.

The KnowHow Book of Puppets

Contents

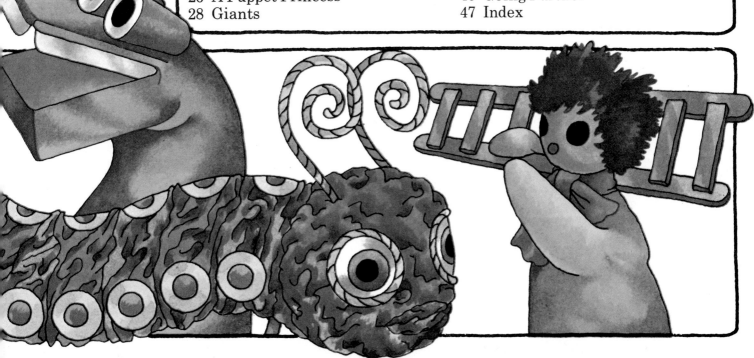

Puppets for Beginners

You will need
a pair of gloves for each puppet
rubber bands and tissue paper
sticky labels
cloth scraps
scissors and strong glue
paints and crayons

Here are three little puppets which are very easy to make. Look at the boxes carefully and you should be able to make them very quickly. The finger mice are called finger puppets. You can make a whole family of mice on the finger tips of one glove. When you've made them, put them on. Put your other hand in front of your palm and make them move up and down behind it.

All the puppets on this page can be used in a puppet play. Have a look at the last six pages of this book and see the kinds of things they can do.

From now on, don't throw anything away. You may be able to make a puppet with it. The most surprising things can be turned into puppets.

Finger Mice

pinch and glue

sticky labels

Cut two ear shapes. Pinch the bottoms with glue. Glue the ears to the fingertip tops. Put on sticky labels for their snouts and eyes. Colour them.

Rabbit

wool

sticky labels

rubber band

scrunched paper stuffing

Turn an old woollen glove inside out. Push the first and little fingers up. Stuff the head with tissue paper. Glue on wool whiskers and sticky label eyes and nose. Use a rubber band for the neck. Put your gloved middle finger into the head. Your thumb and other fingers are legs.

Finger Puppets

Always make finger puppets on the fingertips of whole gloves. It's much easier to put gloves on during a play than lots of tiny puppets.

Spider

rubber band

sticky labels

Put on your gloves. Fix a rubber band around your thumbs. Put sticky labels on the thumbs of your gloves to make spiders' eyes. Now make him move.

The Earth Chief

You will need
a card flower pot
a paper cup
pipe cleaners and beads
2 squeezy bottle tops
sticky labels
scissors and strong glue
a cork bottle top
card and sticky tape
paints and crayons

The Earth Chief Monster puppet
and his private army of Himlings
are not very nice puppets to
know. Their feelers wobble up
and down. Look at the things
they get up to on page 40.

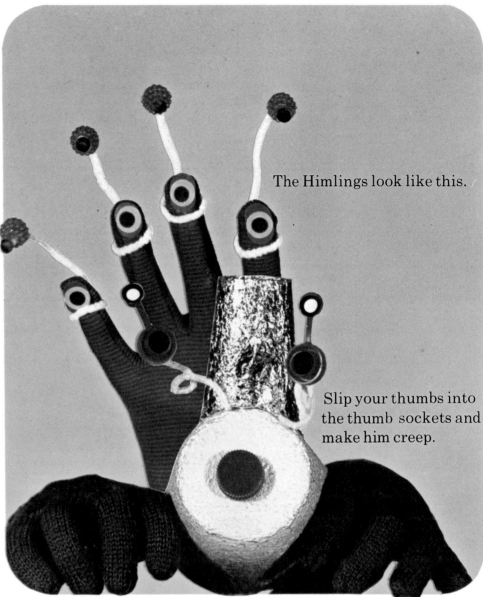

The Himlings look like this.

Slip your thumbs into
the thumb sockets and
make him creep.

1 Making the Earth Chief

twist
push
glue
glue

Twist and curl two pipe cleaners.
Push squeezy bottle tops over the
ends. Glue the other ends to the top
of a card flower pot.

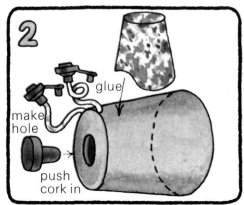

2

glue
make hole
push cork in

Cut a half circle out of a paper cup.
Glue it over the feelers on the front
of the pot. Make a hole in the middle
of the pot and push in a cork bottle
top, so that it looks like this.

3

cut   tape
tape

Cut two bits off the sides of the pot
for your thumbs. Tape two strips of
card each side of the holes to make
thumb sockets. Paint the Earth
Chief now.

Making Himlings

wrap around
push bead over

Twist a pipe cleaner round a glove's
finger tip. Bend it and push a bead
over its top. Do this to each finger
tip. Put sticky labels on for eyes.

Sock Animals and Creatures

You will need
a sock for each puppet
sticky labels for their eyes
For Funny Nose
a sponge for his nose
fur fabric for his hair
a scarf
For a Moose
rubber bands for his ears
scrunched paper to stuff his
   head
strong glue and scissors

Here are three little puppets
you can make from old socks.
Before you use glue have a good
look at the box under here.

Making Slithery Snake

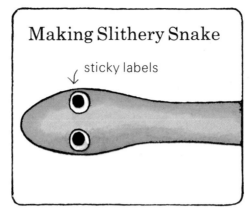

Put a sock over your hand and arm.
Put sticky labels where you think
his eyes look best. Make him wave
up and down over a table.

Rearing Snake

Put your elbow on a table. Put your
arm up straight and bend your hand
over like this.

Look First, Glue Later

When you're sticking on eyes and
hair, just put a little bit of glue on,
see what it looks like, then add
more and glue it down properly.

Making a Moose

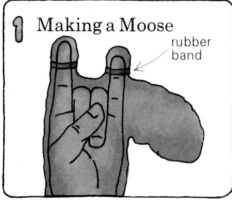

Put your hand into a sock. Poke
two fingers up just after the heel.
Put rubber bands on them. Take
your fingers away and stuff the
rubber band ears with paper.

Stuff the rest of the sock in front
of his ears with crumpled paper.
Put sticky labels where you think
his eyes look best.

Making Funny Nose

Put a sock over your hand and arm.
Put your thumb in the heel so that
it pokes out under the foot of the
sock like this.

Push in the front of the sock to
make a hole. Cut a sponge into a
pear shape. Glue it into the hole.
Stick fur fabric on for his hair and
sticky labels for eyes.

Grinning Funny Nose

Move your thumb down and wiggle
it to and fro.

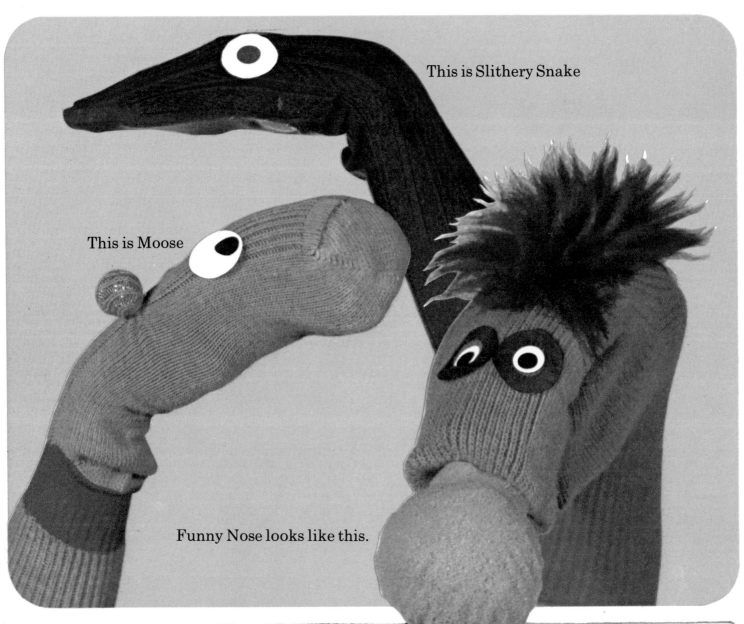

This is Slithery Snake

This is Moose

Funny Nose looks like this.

Thoughtful Funny Nose

Scrunch your hand into a ball and he looks very worried.

Old Lady Funny Nose

Put a scarf over Funny Nose's head and he turns into a very old lady.

Disguise your Voice

Make your mouth into a strange shape. Keep it like that and start to talk. You can't help sounding different when you talk.

Joey the Clown

You will need
a paper plate or card for his
    head
sponge for his nose
cloth for his dress
a ruler for his body
thick wool for his hair
a small strip of card
scissors and strong glue
sticky tape
paints and crayons

This little clown has a magic
neck. When you've made him,
hold his dress, push the ruler
up and his neck will grow
longer and longer.

Making Joey the Clown

cut
sponge

hole

push

wool

Cut out a sponge nose (page 14).
Make a hole in the centre of a paper
plate or card circle, push the nose
in, draw the rest of his face and glue
on wool hair.

This is Joey.

2

tape

small hole   push

cloth

Snip a hole just big enough to
slip the ruler through in the
middle of the cloth. Slip the
ruler through it and tape the
ruler to the back of his head.

Wandering Puppets

Puppets travelled all over the
world. Wandering puppet showmen
would carry their puppets from
country to country, town to town.

They would set up their booths, call
all the people to come and watch,
give a show and then move on to the
next town.

All about Punch and Judy

In some countries, like England, Punch has been bashing puppets on the head for centuries. In other countries, like Germany, he takes the side of law and order. But, whatever he is doing, nearly every country has its Punch. You can see him in France and Germany, in Italy where he came from and in Russia. If you want a Punch puppet, you will have to ask someone to buy you one, or you will have to make one. Punch is a glove puppet, so have a look at the pages on glove puppets in this book.

1 Punch and Judy Story

Punch dances around singing to himself. Judy comes on and asks him to look after the baby. But the baby won't stop crying, so he throws the baby away.

Judy wants to know where the baby has gone. The audience says he has thrown it out of the window. She gets a stick. He grabs it, throws her after the baby and rides off.

Punch falls off his horse and calls for a Doctor. He kicks the Doctor in the eye and the Doctor gets a stick. Punch grabs it and knocks the Doctor out of the way.

A policeman, an Officer and Jack Ketch, the Hangman, come on to arrest Punch for murder. After a fight they get the better of him and drag him off to jail.

Instead of Punch getting hung for three murders, he manages to get Jack Ketch to put his head into the noose, pulls the rope and hangs Jack Ketch instead.

On comes the Devil brandishing a stick. After chatting for a bit they have a great duel which Punch wins and he whirls the Devil around on top of his stick.

Swazzles

Punch and Judy men put a Swazzle into their mouths. They force their breath through the swazzle and their voices sound squeaky. This is how they get Punch's hooting voice.

Punch's Birthday Cake

In 1962 Punch and Judy men gave a huge birthday party for Punch to celebrate his 300th year in England. Snakes and dragons came out of his cake.

9

Boy and Girl Glove Puppets

You will need
2 bits of cloth twice as big as
your hand and forearm
an artificial sponge for her
a sock for him
cardboard for their necks
fur fabric
different material for her hair
old tights or cotton wool
needle and thread
scissors
paper and a pencil
a ruler
strong glue
sticky labels
paints and crayons

Making Bodies

knot and stitch

Cut round it. Turn the cloth bits
the other way round and sew them
together with tiny stitches. Pull it
inside out. Now its inside's the
outside.

Making the Girl's Head

glue — snip hole

dab glue

Make a card tube which is thinner
at the top. Snip a hole in the sponge
large and deep enough for half the
tube. Glue the tube into the sponge
hole like this.

Making Bodies

2 cm

4 cm

2 cm

unfold

3 cm

cut

draw

pin

Fold a long piece of paper and put
your second finger on the fold like
this. Draw round your hand and
forearm as far down as your elbow.
Measure and mark where shown
and join the marks up. Cut it out,
unfold it and pin to a double layer of
cloth as shown.

1 Making the Boy's Head

stuff sock loosely

Loosely stuff the foot of a sock
with old tights or cotton wool.
Make a card tube which is thinner
at the top for the neck.

2

tie

cut sock

Use a piece of wool to hold the
stuffing and half the neck tube in
the sock. Then cut the sock off at the
heel like this.

Joining Heads and Bodies

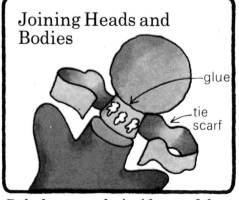

glue

tie scarf

Dab glue on to the inside top of the
body and the bottom of the neck
tube. Glue them both together. Tie
a strip of cloth round the neck to
make it neat.

Making his Hair

sticky labels

Stick fur fabric all over the back of
his head. Use sticky labels, buttons
or felt for his eyes and mouth.

This is what they look like.

Making her Hair

cut

glue

Cut a band of cloth into strips from both sides. Don't cut all the way through the centre. Glue it on to her head. Trim it if it's too long.

1 Making Knots and Stitching 2

Twist the end of a thread twice round your finger. Push the needle under the loops you've made. Pull the thread through, ease the knot off your finger.

Hold the material. Push the needle up through it and then down where your last stitch ended. Keep on doing this. Make the stitches as small as you can.

11

Puppet Action

You will need
your puppets
a yoghurt pot
silver foil
string
scissors and glue
a bundle of small twigs
a larger twig, rod or pencil

Puppet Action is all about giving your puppet life. Once you know how to hold him properly he will do the rest. Just relax and think what kind of character he is.

Don't keep the puppet's arms in the air all the time. Put them up when there's a good reason for it – when your puppet is afraid or surprised, for instance. To make him go to sleep turn his head away and let his head rest on his arms. He can't close his eyes so the only way to show that he's asleep is to hide his face.

Holding a Puppet

Put your middle fingers into the puppet's neck. Your two end fingers go in one arm. Your thumb goes in the other. This is the proper way to hold him.

Making a Bucket

handle   make a hole

push round

glue

Cover a yoghurt pot completely with silver foil. Make two holes with your scissors near the top for a string handle. Tape it in.

Carrying Loads

To make a puppet carry something on his back, bend your middle fingers down and use your other fingers to hold the load behind his head like this.

Just Standing

Bend your thumb and outer fingers on to his chest. We don't stand around with our arms in the air all the time, so why should puppets?

Bowing

Your wrist is the puppet's waist. Bend your whole hand forward and he can bow.

Turning his Neck

Push your two neck fingers hard against the edge of the neck tube. Keep them there. Move your fingers round and he turns his neck.

Making a Broom

glue

glue

tie

Tie some small twigs to one end of a thicker twig or old pencil. Use cotton or thin string to do this.

Using Things

See how many things you can make your puppet do. Give him pens and pencils to play with.

Can you make him carry the bucket and sweep with the broom?

Faces and Hair

On this page there are lots of little tips on how to make different kinds of faces for your puppet. If you look at the boxes carefully you should be able to give your puppet any kind of face you like. You must remember that your friends will be watching from a distance, so always use bright colours. Don't worry about too much detail either. It won't show up from far away and it takes a long time to do. Can you think of any other odds and ends that would made good faces?

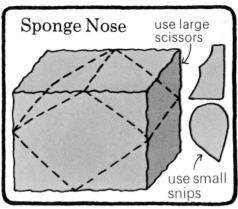

Sponge Nose

use large scissors

use small snips

Cut the nose shape with large sharp scissors. Then trim it with small scissors. Use small snips at a time. Try different nose shapes.

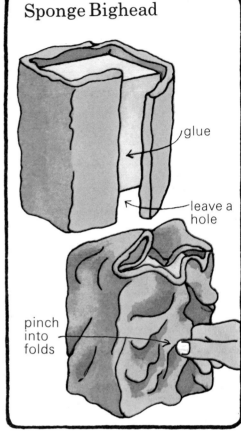

Sponge Bighead

glue

leave a hole

pinch into folds

Glue a sheet of sponge to an old box. Immediately slide, push and pinch the sponge to make folds of skin. The glue must still be wet. Even plastic containers will do. You can make really good wrinkles like this. (See page 46 on what glue to use.)

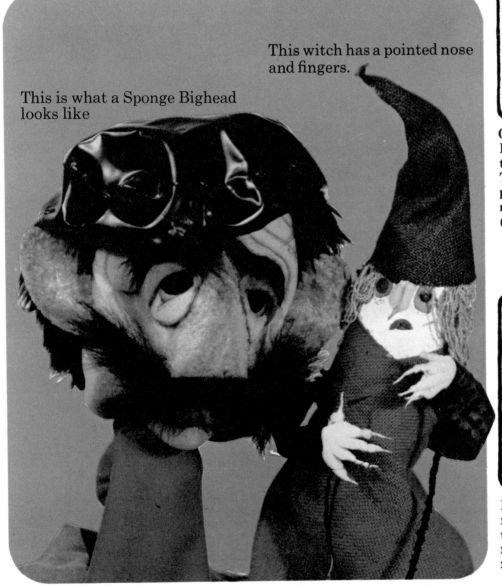

This is what a Sponge Bighead looks like

This witch has a pointed nose and fingers.

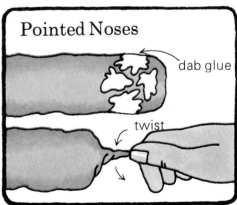

Pointed Noses

dab glue

twist

Dab the end of a sponge nose with a rubber solution glue. Pinch and twist it between your thumb and fingers to make it pointed. Make fingers too.

You can make this little pig by giving him a sponge face, nose and ears. His eyes are made from buttons.

Wool Hair

1 Paper clip some wool or tape along the top of a long piece of card. It must be twice as long as the card. Wind more wool round tightly. Dab glue on top.

2 Knot the top strand. Cut all the way along the bottom. Dab glue along the top again and press down the knotted strand. This will be the puppet's parting.

3 Put glue over the back of the puppet's head. Take the wool hair off the card and press it on to the puppet like this.

Beards and Hair

Scrunch up tissue paper and glue it to the puppet. Fur fabric makes a good beard as well.

Sticking on Hollow Noses

If you want a hollow bottle top nose and you want to stick it to something slippery, glue sponge or crumpled paper into it and trim any paper that sticks out.

Eyes

When you're making eyes, it's a good idea to draw a dark circle around them and to give them a pupil. This makes them show up well from far away.

Tips for Small Puppets

The lower down on a puppet's face that you stick its eyes and mouth, the younger it will look. Small puppets do not always need noses to make them look real.

Mouth Monsters

You will need
For a Cake Box Monster
a cake box and a thimble
2 bits of cloth wide enough to
    wrap a cake box in and as long
    as your arm
2 yoghurt pots for his eyes
paper to cover them
For an Egg Box Monster
2 egg boxes
an old woollen sleeve
2 bottle tops and sticky labels
scissors and glue

Cake Box Monster

Finger Bands

**Tape box hinge. Squash the back
of the box until you can hold it. Cut
two strips of card and glue the strip
ends to the box as shown to make
into finger bands.**

1 Making the Cake Box Monster

Make finger bands. Glue one bit of
cloth to the front and sides of the
box. Glue the other to the front and
sides of the lid. Glue the cloth edges
together.

2

Put paper over the open ends of
two yoghurt pots. Glue it down over
the sides (a). Then cover the sides
with paper (b). Paint a blob on the
other ends (c).

3

Glue the pots to the top of his head.
Stick a thimble to the front of his
head for his nose. Paint the inside
of his mouth.

Floating Monsters

Sometimes there are puppet shows where the puppets and the people who work them are on the stage together. But you can't see the people because they're dressed in black and the background is black

too. All you see are bright and colourful puppets which look as if they're moving by magic. They just float in mid-air. It's called the Black Theatre.

1 Making the Egg Box Monster

finger bands
pull sleeve over

Make finger bands (see opposite page). Shut the box and pull the sleeve of an old woollen jumper right over it until it is completely covered.

Egg Box Monster

2 glue wool into nostrils

glue

cut so that it opens

Cut the wool along the sides of the egg box so that it opens. Glue the cut edges of the wool over the box's sides and front. Pinch and glue the nostrils like this.

3 glue

Cut two egg holders from another egg box and stick a bottle top to the top of each. Glue them to the top of his head and stick labels to the bottle tops for his eyes.

OddFrog and GooseBeak

You will need
For OddFrog
a paper plate or circle of card
some cloth twice as wide as
   the plate and as long as your
   arm
tissue paper and bottle tops
For GooseBeak
card at least 30 cm long and wide
   for his beak
an old shirt for his body
about 4 thin plastic bags
any old hat with a brim
cotton wool
sticky labels and buttons
scissors and strong glue
a needle and thread

1 Making GooseBeak

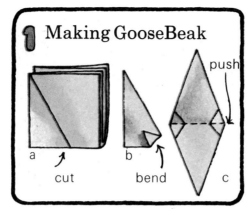

Fold some card in four and cut a
long triangle shape (a). Bend in the
corners (b). Open the card out and
push the corner bends inwards (c).

2

Make finger bands (page 16). Crunch
thin plastic bags into balls. Glue
them to the top and bottom of his
beak like this.

Asking for Help

Let your puppet ask the audience
for help. Hide something and let
them see where you hide it. Then,
get him to ask them where it is.
Make him look in the wrong places.

1 Making OddFrog

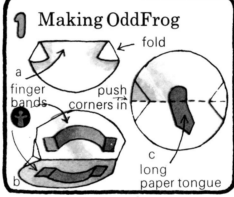

Fold a paper plate in half. Bend the
corners in (a). Open it. Make finger
bands on the outside (page 16) and
push the corners in (b). Stick a paper
tongue inside (c).

2

Put the mouth in the material. Fold
edges over with an overlap and glue
them together. Cut round the curve
of the plate and glue the material
to its top.

3

Scrunch tissue paper as shown.
Glue it to the top of his head. Make
his eyes from bottle tops and sticky
labels. Glue them to the top of his
head like this.

3

glue

glue felt

glue felt

glue felt

Slip a sleeve of an old shirt over the plastic balls and glue. Glue felt over the outsides of his beak. Paint the inside as shown.

4

cut

tuck in and sew

stuff

Cut off half the other sleeve of the old shirt. Sew the sleeve's frayed edges together. Stuff it with cotton wool to make a tail. Tuck in the collar and sew it.

5

glue on cotton wool

cut

cut

Cut two holes for your arms on each side of an old hat. Cover its top and sides, but not the armholes, with cotton wool. Glue the cotton wool on as shown.

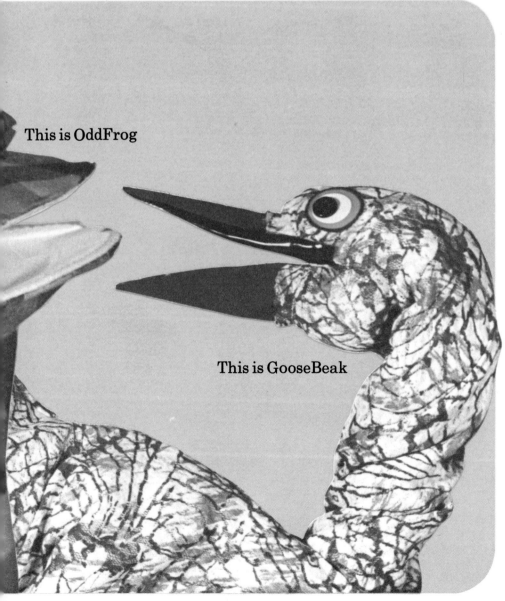

This is OddFrog

This is GooseBeak

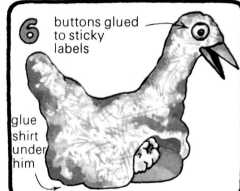

6

buttons glued to sticky labels

glue shirt under him

Pull the shirt down over the hat so that the two hat holes are under the sleeve openings. Glue the shirt's edge under the brim. Stick on eyes as shown.

Working GooseBeak

Cross your arms and keeping them crossed, put one arm through one hole up to his head, put the other arm through the other hole up to his tail. Lift your arms up.

19

Stick Puppet Animals

You will need
1.5 metres of rope
tissue paper for their bodies
a needle, thread and strong glue
scissors and sticky tape

For the Cat
a flat sponge for the cat's head
rubber bands for his whiskers
2 beads, card and safety pins
thin sponge for his ears and nose

For the Wolf
card 30 cm × 60 cm for his head
a rubber glove finger tip for
    his nose
scrunched paper to stuff his jaw
4 straight sticks 1 metre long

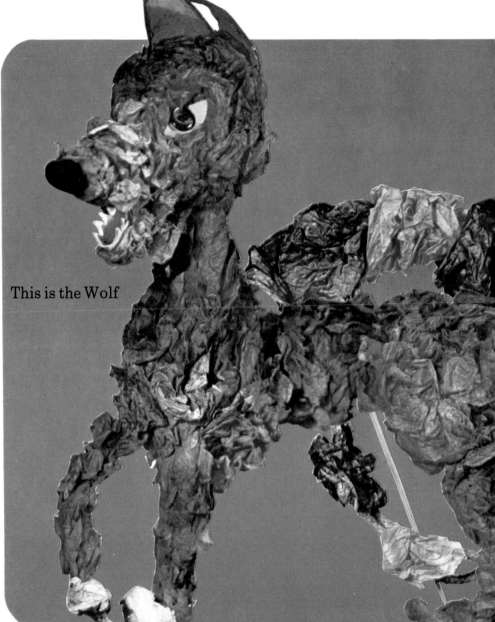

This is the Wolf

1 The Cat's Head

push in and glue

push in and glue

Make two slits in a flat sponge as
shown. Glue the insides of the slits
and stick a straight stick and a
piece of long thick rope in as shown.

Glue rubber band whiskers on to his
face. Stick on sponge nose over
them. Make two slots for his ears
and stick two thin sponge ears into
them.

slot in and glue

glue

The Cat's Wobbly Eyes

tie behind

tie

tape

Loosely thread a bead. Tie some
more thread through a piece of card
and hang the beaded thread from
this. Tape a safety pin on to the
back like this.

Making the Cat's Body

tape

cut

Decide how long you want the body
to be. Tape the rope firmly to a
second straight stick. Cut it off at
the end for its tail.

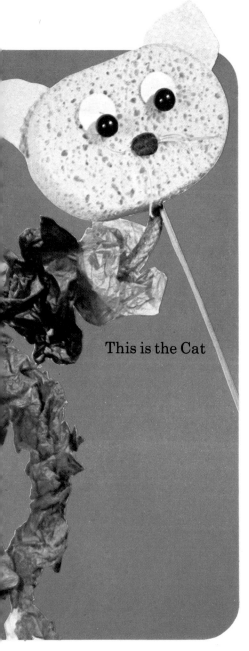

This is the Cat

1 Making the Wolf

Fold some card. Draw a wolf's head shape, a pointed ear and a jaw. Cut them out where shown. Unfold them and cut the ear only along the fold.

2

tape

tape to here

bend

Tape the back of the head shape to a straight stick. Bend the sides of the shape round. Tape half the shape together. Tape ears to the back of the head.

3

tape   tape

Tape the two ends of the jaw. Stuff it with a little bit of scrunched paper. Tape it firmly to the straight stick just under the head shape.

Making the Wolf's Body

tape

Make his body like the cat's. Cut two bits of rope and tape one to each straight stick as shown. Cover the ropes and sticks with tissue paper like the cat.

Papering the Cat's Body

wrap and glue

Scrunch and twist long strips of tissue paper. Wind the paper strips round the rope leaving a bit of rope free near the head for the neck. Glue the strips to the rope.

Sitting Wolf

Tie a string loop to the bottom of his rope back paw. Hold the back stick and put one of the fingers from the same hand through the loop. Move them up as shown.

Prancing Wolf

push rope up

Tie some rope to his rope front paw. Hold the front stick and push the rope you've just tied on up and out with the fingers of the same hand.

21

Caterpillars that Creep and Twist

You will need
rope about 1 metre long
3 straight sticks 1 metre long
white card 20 cm × 20 cm
2 paper cups
2 bottle tops
a pipe cleaner
stiff white paper
a broom handle or pencil
lots of sticky labels
sticky tape and a stapler
scissors and strong glue
a ruler
scrunched up paper

Shadow Puppets

There are puppet shows in the Far East called Shadow Shows. The puppets are made of very thin parchment. They are put between a screen and a bright light. The light throws the puppet's shadow on to the screen. It can be seen by the audience which sits on the other side of the screen. People can make them do amazing things like jumping and suddenly disappearing.

Creeping Caterpillar

22

1 Making the Caterpillar

Fold the white card. Draw a caterpillar's head shape with tabs at its back. Cut it out, but not along the fold. Bend the tabs along the tab line.

2

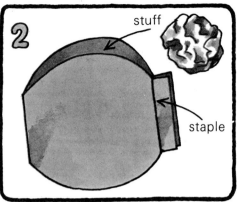

Staple the shape together along the tab line. Scrunch paper into balls and stuff them into the head shape.

3

Tape the rope to the top of the three sticks as shown. Push the first stick into the head shape's tabs. Bend the tabs over the stick and staple it in as shown.

4

Cover the whole rope by winding and gluing long strips of scrunched up tissue paper along it. Put sticky labels down both sides of the paper.

5

Glue on paper cup eyes and curly feelers. Twist a pipe cleaner into a ring and glue a paper strip round it. Glue it around the paper cup eyes.

Making Paper Cup Eyes

Cut the top off a paper cup at a slant. Make downward cuts along its rim and bend them out. Dab glue on the insides of the cuts. Glue the cups to the puppet's head. Make pupils with sticky labels. Stick them to bottle tops. Glue these to the cups.

Making Curly Feelers and Curls

Wind thin strips of stiff paper tightly around a pencil. (For big curls use a broom handle.) Then slip the paper off.

You can make curls another way by holding the ruler and paper as shown. Push the ruler along the paper and the paper will curl.

Captain Plunder Bones

You will need

a medium sized cereal packet
a cardboard tube from a kitchen
 roll
a thick stick about 60 cm long
an old T-shirt
2 straight sticks 1 metre long
2 old stockings
card for ears, eye patch and hands
a scarf and old curtain ring
fur fabric or wood shavings
a cork for his nose
scissors and string
strong glue and sticky tape

Captain Plunder Bones is a three
stick puppet. Make him nice and
big. Make the hand sticks first.

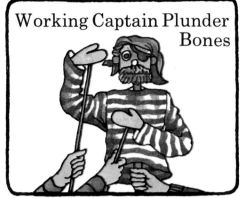

Working Captain Plunder Bones

Captain Plunder Bones is better
if two of you work him. One the
main stick, the other the hand
sticks. Stand facing each other.

Speaking and Moving

The person working the main stick
speaks for the puppet. He also turns
the puppet's head and moves the
puppet from one part of the stage
to another.

Making Card Ears

glue

cut

these are
the tabs

Fold some card. Cut out two ear
shapes with tabs as shown. Bend
the tabs out. Glue the two ear
shapes together, but not the tabs.
Glue tabs on to the puppet.

Making Hand Sticks

unbend

dab
glue

wind
tightly

Hand sticks move the puppet's
hands. Unbend a paper clip. Put it
on top of a straight stick and glue
and wind string round them both
very tightly.

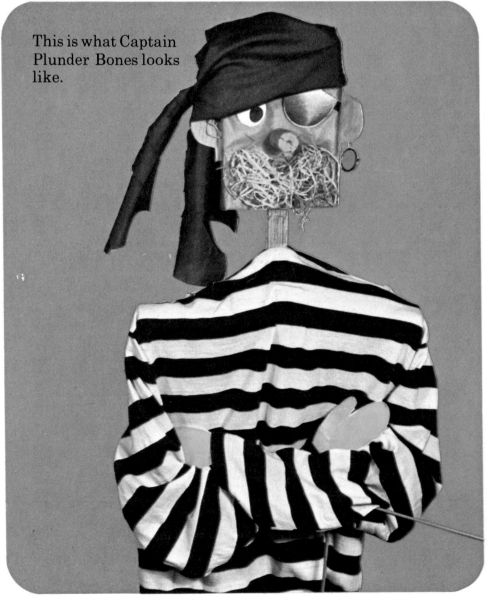

This is what Captain
Plunder Bones looks
like.

Reaching Up

Hold the puppet up high. You must always remember to make the hand sticks long enough for him to reach right above his head without your arms being seen.

Holding the Hand Sticks

If you move his hand sticks behind his back, his arms will look as if they're broken. Keep them in front of him or at his sides.

Working him Alone

If you tilt the main stick forward so that his arms fall in front of him, you won't have to hold the hand sticks. You can work them one at a time then.

1 Making Captain Plunder Bones

tape

Cut off the bottom of the cereal packet. Tape a thick stick firmly down the centre of the inside of the packet. This is the main stick.

2

glue

glue and tape

Glue and tape a kitchen roll tube behind the thick stick as shown. Glue an old stocking to each end of the tube. These will be his arms.

3

cover or paint

Cover or paint the cereal packet with one colour. Dress him in an old T-shirt. Always remember to dress stick puppets before you put their hands on.

4

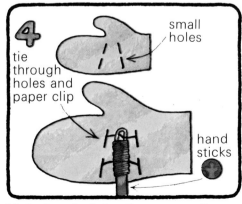

small holes

tie through holes and paper clip

hand sticks

Make hand sticks. Cut two card hand shapes. Make four little holes as shown. Put a hand stick between them and tie string through them and the paper clip.

5

Roll up the T-shirt sleeves. Glue and tape the ends of the stockings to the hands like this. Roll the sleeves down again to hide the joins.

6

scarf

patch

card ears

sticky labels

cork nose

fur fabric

Glue on a cork nose, card ears and a fur fabric or wood shaving beard. Give him a scarf, a black patch and an ear ring made from an old curtain ring like this.

A Puppet Princess

You will need

white card 40 cm × 20 cm for her
   face
a cardboard kitchen tube
2 hand sticks (page 24)
1 metre of cloth for her dress
1 metre of rope for her arms
white card for her hands
stiff black paper for her hair
coloured cord for her dress
scissors and strong glue
a needle and thread
sticky tape
paints and crayons

This puppet has hand sticks like
Captain Plunder Bones. Her
hands move in a very beautiful way.

Bend the white card round so that
the ends overlap each other at the
back and are higher than at the
front (a). Tape it and trim off any
overlap at the back (b).

Tape a cardboard kitchen tube up
the middle of the face shape (a). If
you do it properly the face shape
should tip down a bit (b).

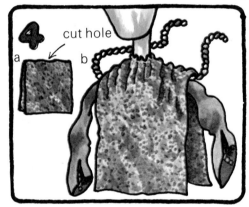

Fold her dress material in half.
Make a hole in the middle (a). Push
the main stick and arms through
the hole. Put coloured cord under
dress as shown (b).

Sew down the sides of the dress.
Knot the coloured cord gently
behind the main rod. Tie some more
cord loosely round her waist and
glue it to the dress.

Cut out two white card hands 20 cm
long. Tape a paper clip near the
wrist of each (a). Make hand sticks
(page 24) and fix them to the paper
clip as shown. (b).

Glue stiff black paper to the back
and sides of her head. Cut some
more black paper into long strips
and curl them (page 23). Stick
curled strips to her head.

Fold some card and cut out her
crown (a). Glue it into a circle and
slip it on to her head. Draw her face
with a felt pen. Glue on eyelids and
eyelashes as shown. (b).

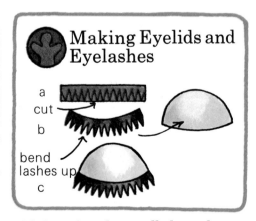

Making Eyelids and Eyelashes

Make pointed cuts all along the
bottom of a very thin strip of stiff
paper (a). Bend the cuts up into
lashes (b). Then glue it on to a card
eyelid like this. (c).

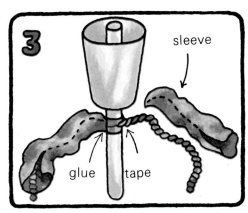

3

sleeve

glue tape

Tape rope arms to the main stick. Sew together two sleeves leaving an opening at the bottom. Pull them over the rope and glue them to the main stick as shown.

7

tape

bend

bend

a

b

leave slit for hand stick

Bend the sides of the wrist a bit and tape the hands to the rope arms (a). Sew the rest of the sleeve together leaving a long slit for the hand stick as shown. (b).

If you get tired

tape

broom

If your arms start to ache when you're working her in a play, you can tape the main stick to a broom as shown.

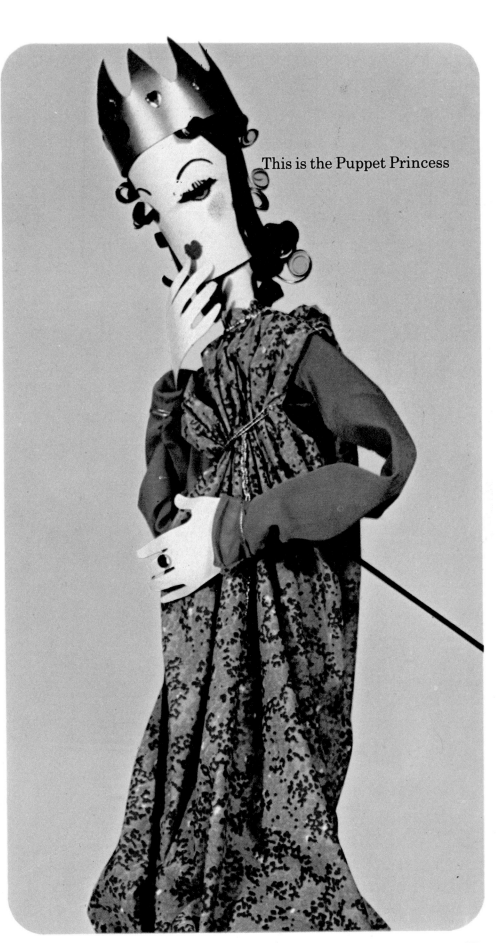

This is the Puppet Princess

Giants

You will need
For the Giant
a big cardboard box for his head
a thick stick 1 metre long
a cardboard kitchen tube
old stockings for hair
3 paper cups
1 metre of cloth for his clothes
For a Megaphone
thick card 40 cm × 20 cm
For a Treasure Trove
an old box
silver foil and coloured paper
a needle and thread
scissors and sticky tape
strong glue

Making a Giant card ears
paint
paper cup eyes and nose

Cut the bottom off the box. Tape the thick stick up the inside of it and paint the box. Glue on a paper cup nose and eyes (page 23) and card ears (page 24).

make little cuts
old stockings
push tube up
tape

Glue scrunched up old stockings on to his head and under his nose and make little cuts in them. Slip a cardboard tube up the stick, wind tape under it to keep it up.

Working the Giant

You need a helper to work the Giant. Get the helper to put his thumbs into the thumb loops. It'll look as if they're the Giant's hands.

Twisting his Neck

If you twist the stick with one hand and hold the tube without twisting it with the other, he will turn his head without moving his body.

This is the Giant

3 Fold the material you're going to dress him in into four. Cut a hole as shown. Make two marks on the top end of each fold with a felt pen as shown.

4 Thread a needle and make two thread loops. Put them on the felt pen marks. You work the Giant's hands by putting your own thumbs through the loops.

5 Push the stick and tube down through the hole in the middle of the material. Glue the material round the hole to the tube and tie a scarf round it.

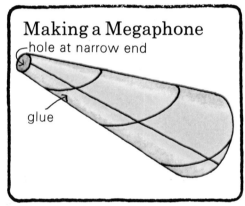

Making a Megaphone

Glue the card for the megaphone into a cone shape. Leave a hole at its narrowest end. Giants have deep, booming voices. Speak down it. Your voice will be loud.

Wellington Boot Giant

If you want to show Giant's feet in a play, put some big boots on to the stage. Other puppets will be much smaller and your Giant will look very big.

Treasure Trove

Paint an old box. Fill it with scrunched up silver foil and coloured paper.

Be a Giant

There's no reason why you should not dress up as a giant yourself and act with the puppets in the play.

Giant Puppets

An American called Remo Bufano made giant puppets. One clown he made was 11 metres high. Some of his puppets were worked from a platform 13 metres up.

Backstage KnowHow

Stage Front

moon on a stick

this is called the playboard

The play has just started. Look at the front of the stage. That's what the audience sees. Look at the picture just below it. This is what it looks like back stage just before a play starts. The puppets are hanging ready and everything that is needed is in its own special place. When you put plays on, you must try to have everything ready like this too.

You will need
4 thick poles 2.5 metres long
4 chairs and some rope
2 sheets and drawing pins

Back Stage

lights

lights

place for sound effects

plank across chairs for putting things

place for props

puppet hook

puppets hanging from rope

Stage Plan

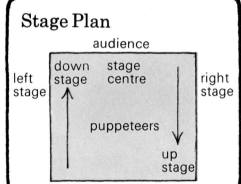

audience

left stage

down stage

stage centre

right stage

puppeteers

up stage

Real puppeteers often use written stage plans on bits of paper to help them remember where puppets are supposed to be.

Puppet Hook and Line

rope taped to front poles

sew on hook

It's a good idea to make a hook from an unbent paper clip sewn to the hem of a puppet's dress. Then you can hook him to a rope taped across the front poles.

Making a Stage for Hand and Stick Puppets

For String Puppets

Tie four poles to four chairs as shown. Stretch the top of an old sheet across the two front poles just above your head. Pin it to the poles as shown.

Pin the top of another sheet to the top of one of the back poles. Stretch it across to the other back pole and pin it to the top of that one. Stand in the middle.

Turn the whole stage round so that the lower sheet is now at the back. Lower this sheet and re-pin it so that you can work a string puppet over it easily.

Scenery

Lights

If you have scenery, don't make it too complicated or people won't be able to see your puppets clearly in a play.

For hand and stick puppets, put your lights each side of the front of the stage pointing towards it. Look at it on the audience side to make sure it's

bright enough. For string puppets put the lights between the sheets pointing on to the puppets. Don't put your stage in front of a window.

Hold them High

Even Higher

Talking to Each Other

Always hold the puppets up high on stage. If you work them so that their hem lines are about $2\frac{1}{2}$ cm below the playboard they will be just the right height.

The further away from the front of the stage you hold your puppet, the higher up you're going to have to hold him.

If your puppets are having a conversation with each other, you must make them face each other. Hold one on each hand.

KnowHow Special Effects Department

Sound Effects are very exciting because they sound so real. But don't use them too much. Real puppeteers only use them when they're needed to make a play more alive.

Anything a puppet uses in a play is called a prop. Don't worry if a puppet drops a prop over the front, make him ask one of the audience for it back.

You will need
card 60 cm × 30 cm for the boat
a straight stick 60cm long
scissors and strong glue

Horses' Hooves

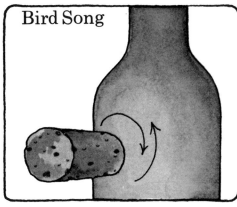

Knock first one side and then the other of two empty yoghurt pots on to the top of a table. Clop one pot after the other and get faster and faster.

Bird Song

Wet a cork and rub it over the side of a glass bottle. Then you can get a chirpy bird song effect.

Crackle of Flames

Crumple cellophane paper into a ball and it'll sound as if there is a large fire nearby.

Thunder

Take a large sheet of card or tin and shake it violently backwards and forwards. It'll sound as if there's a terrible storm outside.

Rain

Sprinkle uncooked rice on to a tin or baking tray. It'll sound as if rain is beating against the window.

Eerie Lights

Cover the front of your stage lights with coloured cellophane. Make sure that it doesn't touch the bulb. The whole of your stage set will change colour.

Marching Feet

Fill a tin with stones. Put the lid back on and shake it up and down. If you put a lot of stones in, it'll sound as if there's a really big army approaching.

Handling Things

Puppets can use almost anything they like as a prop. But make sure they're not too slippery. Be sure they're big enough, too, or they won't be seen.

Making a Boat

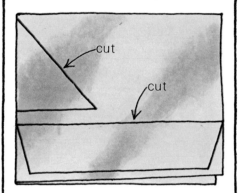

Fold a piece of card. Draw a boat shape and sail. Cut them out. Do not cut the sail along the fold.

Glue a stick to the end of one of the boat shapes. Lay the other one on top and glue them together at both ends. Glue the sail around the top of the stick.

A Puppet Going for a Boat Ride

Hand Puppet Props

When your puppet has to put a prop down during a play, try holding it for him like this.

Stick Puppet Props

Stick puppet props have to go on sticks as well. You will have to be careful to move both together at the same speed.

Going on a Boat Ride

Hold the boat stick in one hand and push the puppet up through the middle of the boat. Then move them both along.

The Serpent and the Phantom Wafter

These are string puppets. Sometimes people call them marionettes. They are worked from above.

You will need
For the Phantom Wafter
1 metre of almost transparent cloth for his body
2 hangers
For the Serpent
about 30 paper cups
about 30 buttons or beads
a thin hollow plastic ball
2 bottle tops and sticky labels
2 hangers
a needle and some strong thread
strong glue and sticky tape

1 Making the Phantom Wafter

Cut four threads 1 m long. Tie three to three of the cloth's corners. Tie the fourth thread to the cloth 6 cm underneath the centre thread as shown.

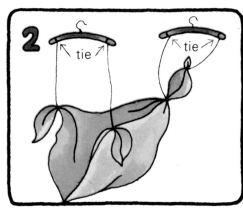

2

Tie the ends of the two side threads to a hanger as shown. Tie the two middle threads to another hanger as shown. When you're not using it hang it up.

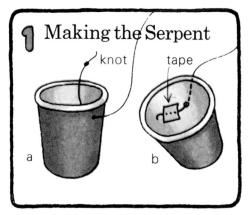

1 Making the Serpent

Thread a needle with 1 m of thread. Knot it. Push the needle through a side of a paper cup (a). Tape the knot (b). Do same again with another cup and thread.

2

Thread a needle with 6 m of double thread. Knot. Push it through the bottom of another cup from the inside. Tape. Push it through a bead, cup, bead, cup 30 times.

3

cups with thread at end and centre of body

Thread the two cups with thread in them to the line of cups and beads. Put one near the end and one in the middle. See that their strings are on the same side.

4

knot

thread with Giant needle

Make two holes on opposite sides of the ball. Make a Giant needle. Thread the two strands through the holes and on through a button or bead. Tie knot as shown.

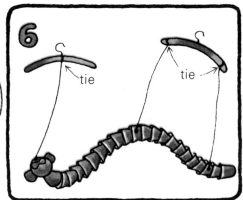

5

paper cup eyes

Glue on paper cup eyes (page 23) decorated with bottle tops and sticky labels. Make a big bow and glue it between the eyes as shown.

6

tie — tie

Tie the thread that comes out of the head to the middle of one hanger. Tie the two threads in the cups to different ends of another hanger as shown.

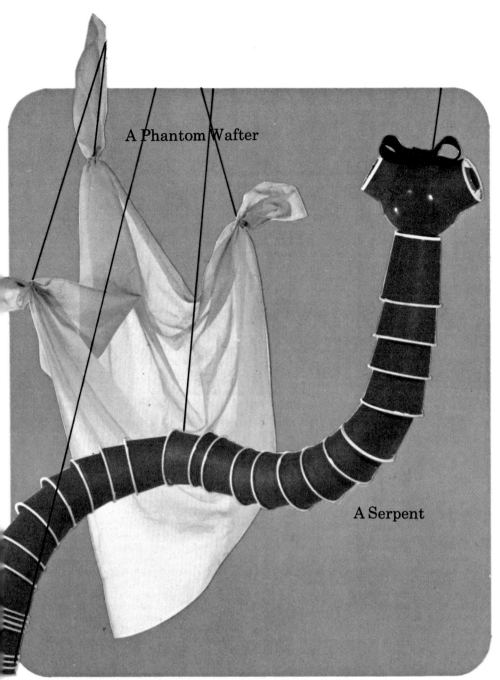

A Phantom Wafter

A Serpent

1 Making a Serpent Slither

head hanger

cup on its open end

Hold the hangers in different hands. Tip the body hanger down and make the end cup stand on its open end as shown.

2

Gently lower the rest of his cup body on to the bottom cup. Bring the head hanger towards the body hanger. Move the hanger up and he comes out again.

Battling Puppets

There are puppeteers in Sicily who use puppets dressed in shining armour like these puppets here. The puppet plays show the adventures of medieval knights.

They fight great duels and battles. Even St. George appears with a dragon belching fire and smoke.

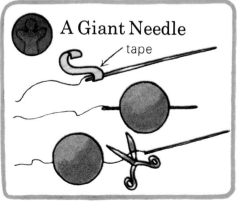

A Giant Needle

tape

If you want to pass a thread through something that is wider than the length of your needle, tape the thread to a piece of wire, push through and cut.

Little Girl Marionette

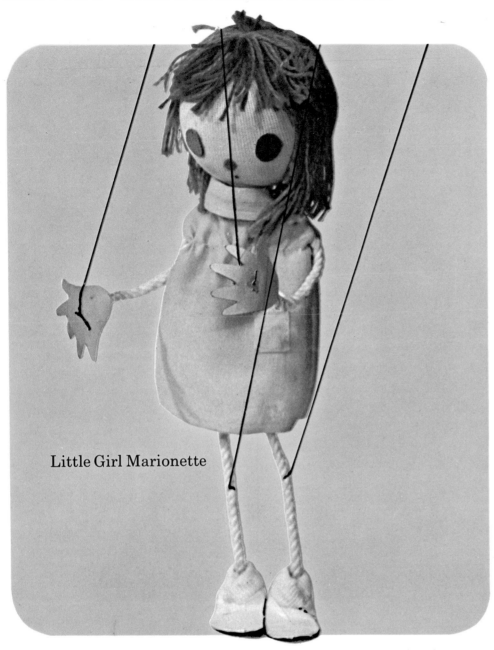

Little Girl Marionette

You will need
For the Little Girl
a small cardboard box 8 cm × 5 cm
50 cm of white rope
an old stocking
a hollow plastic ball 8 cm wide
cloth for her dress
card for hands, feet and neck
wool and sticky labels
plasticine and coloured tape
For her Control
card from the back of a writing
　　pad
4 small corks and 4 screw eyes
For them both
florist's wire
paper clips
scissors, glue and sticky tape

Cut off the rest of the sock. Make
a card neck tube. Cut a hole in the
ball big enough for the neck tube.
Glue neck tube up into her head
and down into her body.

This is what her Control looks
like

1 Making the Control

Make three card tubes big enough
to put corks into (a). Paint them
as shown. Push corks into the ends
of two of the tubes. Twist screw
eyes into the corks (b).

Cut three bits of wire, two as long
as a tube (a), the other more than
twice as long. Bend the long wire
double, push and tape it up a tube,
bend it into a hook (b).

1 Making the Marionette

hole for neck
hole for arm
tape
paper clip
cut front and back flaps

Cut the bottom flaps of the box as shown. Cut out arm and neck holes. Tape a paper clip hook to the bottom of the box. This is for the back string.

2

push rope
glue
glue

Push two strands of rope through each armhole, down the inside of the box and out at the other end. Glue them inside the box. Glue bottom box flaps together again.

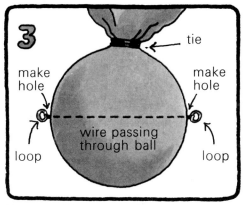

3

tie
make hole
make hole
wire passing through ball
loop
loop

Put a ball inside the foot of a sock. Tie sock tightly at the top of the ball. Make two holes each side of the ball. Push a wire through the holes. Twist it into loops.

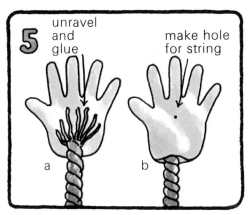

5

unravel and glue
make hole for string
a
b

Cut out four hand shapes. Unravel the ends of the rope arms a bit so they lie flat. Glue them to the hand shapes (a). Glue another shape on top. Make a hole (b).

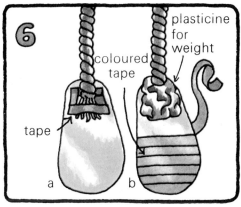

6

plasticine for weight
coloured tape
tape
a
b

Cut out two foot shapes. Unravel the rope leg ends and tape them to the foot shapes (a). Put some plasticine over the joins. Cover each foot with coloured tape.

7 Hair, Face and Clothes

Dress her (page 27, the Princess's dress). Glue on wool hair (page 15) and painted card eyes, a felt nose and draw her mouth. Colour her cheeks.

3

tape
loop
a
loop
b
tape hook
push

Make four holes near the top of the tube. Push the smaller wires through the holes. Loop the wire ends (a). Tape a paper clip hook to the tube's lower end (b).

4

extra wire
bend and tape

Bend the extra wire at the end of this tube around the middle of one of the other tubes. Tape the join to make it stronger.

5

paper clip hook
hang it over wire hook
tape

Make another paper clip hook and tape it to the middle of the remaining tube. Hang this tube by its hook over the tube with the wire hook at the end of it.

Stringing and Working the Marionette

1 Stringing the Puppet

leg string here
leg string here
arm strings at end of arm bars
head string here
head string here
back string here

This is where you tie the puppet strings. Ask a helper to hold either the puppet or the control. Use strong carpet thread the whole time. Dab glue over your knots.

2 Head Strings

Ask a helper to hold her with her feet on the floor. Hold the control just above your waist. Tie thread from the wire loops on her head to

the screw eyes on the head bar as shown. She should be able to stand up straight now. Make her stand while you tie on her strings.

3 Back String

Cut a hole in her dress on top of the paper clip hook on her back. Ask a helper to hold the control at waist level. Tie thread from the hook on her back up to the back string hook.

4 Leg Strings

Tie the leg strings to her legs at the point you think her knees should be. Tie the other end to the screw eyes on the leg bar.

5 Hand Strings

Let her hands hang and push the hand strings through the holes in her hands and tie. Tie the other end of the thread to the arm bars.

Standing Still

Hold the centre bar firmly in one hand so that her feet just touch the floor. Don't let the strings get too loose or she'll look as if she's going to faint.

Hands Up

Still with one hand, put your thumb under one arm bar and your forefinger under the other. You can make her lift her hands by moving your thumb and finger up.

Waving

Here's another way to make her move her hands. Lift one of the hand strings with your other hand and make her wave.

Little Girl Marionette

One Leg Up

Unhook the leg bar and hold it as shown. Tip it so that it points down and she will raise one of her legs. Tipping it the other way moves the other leg.

Going for a Walk

Hold the leg bar in front of the main bar. Rock it up and down, moving both bars forward at the same speed. Make her turn and change her direction.

Bowing

Lift the back string with one hand and with the other move the control forwards. Don't move it forwards too far or her legs will leave the floor and she'll fly.

Sitting

Make sure that she's got her feet firmly on the ground. Then just lower the control without moving it backwards or forwards and she sits down. Now make her stand up.

Putting her Away

When you put her away, twist her body round and round until all the strings are joined together. Then you won't get into a mess untangling her strings later.

The Invasion of the Earth Chief

Scene 1

The Girl is crying because she's lost her goose. Her brother, the Boy says he'll go and look for it.

Scene 2

He looks for it everywhere. At last he finds it. It was hiding. 'I can't even hide in peace. Don't you know that they're coming?' says Goose. 'Who are?' asks the Boy, very puzzled. They hear a noise.

Scene 3

Rabbit comes on crying for help. 'I'm covered with the Himlings' sticky stuff. If I don't get it off I'll die,' says Rabbit. 'My sister will wash it off,' says the Boy.

Scene 4

They wash him. 'The Earth Chief is wandering around. He has a strange ship and an army of Himlings. He sniffs the air with his wobbly feelers,' says Rabbit.

Scene 5

Suddenly they hear an eerie sniffing sound. 'Hide. It must be the Earth Chief' says Rabbit. They hide behind a rock just as the Earth Chief comes on with his Himling Army behind him.

Scene 6

'What's happening?' cries the Boy. 'I'm being moved towards it. I can't stop. Help.' The Earth Chief sends out his thought waves and the Boy is dragged nearer and nearer the Earth Chief's ship ....
(*Finish the story your way.*)

If you have never put on a puppet play before, you might like to base your first play on one of the three stories we have here and on the next few pages. We only give you half stories. They all stop at an exciting point in the story. What you have to do is to make up the ending yourselves.

Do not let too many people work the puppets at the same time, or you will bump into each other. You must have room to turn round in. Have the puppets and props ready (page 30). Decide who is going to work each puppet. Decide what is going to happen in each scene and what each puppet is going to say. Write it down. When you have done a few plays you will not have to write everything down.

This is a story about what happens to a little girl, her brother, Goose and Rabbit when the Earth Chief Monster invades the Earth with his army of Himlings and captures the Boy with his powerful thought waves. Make up the end of the story of how the little girl and her friends outwit the Monster. You will find the Earth Chief and his Himling Army on page 5, Little Girl and Boy on page 10, Rabbit on page 4, Goose on page 18.

Making a Programme

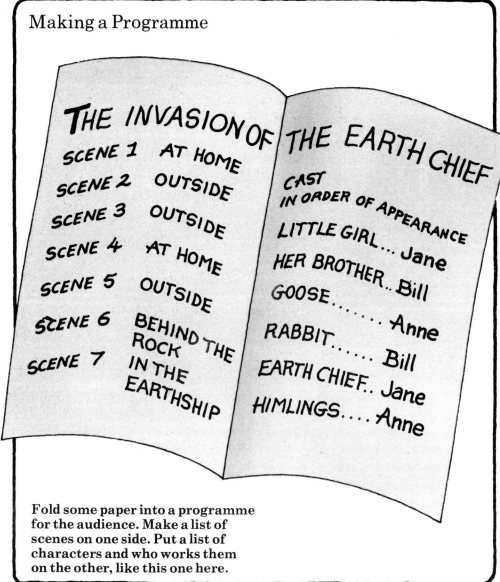

THE INVASION OF THE EARTH CHIEF

SCENE 1   AT HOME
SCENE 2   OUTSIDE
SCENE 3   OUTSIDE
SCENE 4   AT HOME
SCENE 5   OUTSIDE
SCENE 6   BEHIND THE ROCK
SCENE 7   IN THE EARTHSHIP

CAST
IN ORDER OF APPEARANCE
LITTLE GIRL... Jane
HER BROTHER.. Bill
GOOSE........ Anne
RABBIT....... Bill
EARTH CHIEF.. Jane
HIMLINGS..... Anne

Fold some paper into a programme for the audience. Make a list of scenes on one side. Put a list of characters and who works them on the other, like this one here.

Having a Good Wash

The person working the Girl can blow bubbles with her free hand from underneath the stage front. Someone else has the Boy on one hand and Rabbit on the other.

Advancing and Sniffing

The person who worked the Girl now works the Earth Chief with both hands. You'll need another helper to work the Himlings.

Sticky Stuff

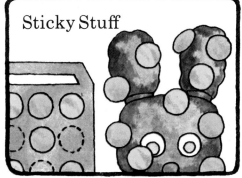

Cover Rabbit with coloured sticky labels. The Boy will be able to pull them off easily and then stick them to something else under the stage.

The Princess and the Magic Potion

'I don't know what to do about my daughter. She never laughs,' says the King to the Doctor. 'Let me examine her and I'll see if I can find a cure,' says the Doctor.

'Joey's the funniest clown in the world. He'll make her laugh,' who says. So Joey comes, he dances, tells jokes, makes his neck grow and grow. But the Princess still doesn't laugh.

One day, the Princess finds a big caterpillar in the garden. 'Where do you come from?' she asks. 'I fell out of a giant's sandwich,' says Caterpillar. She asks him if he can make her laugh.

'The Giant has a magic potion in his castle. That'll cure you,' says Caterpillar. They go in search of him. Suddenly they hear a booming sound. 'It's the Giant,' they say.

The Giant seizes the Princess. 'Just what I need for my supper. I'll pick some lettuce too,' he says. Caterpillar hides in a lettuce leaf. The Giant picks it and marches off.

The Giant puts the Princess in his deepest dungeon and leaves a guard dog monster to see that she doesn't escape. He goes off to have his sandwich . . . .
(*Finish the story your way.*)

This is a story about a Princess who cannot laugh. She goes in search of the magic laughing potion but is captured by the Giant who keeps it. Will she escape and find the potion? The ending is for you to decide. You will find the Puppet Princess on page 26, Caterpillar on page 22, Giant on page 28, Joey the Clown on page 8, Guard Dog Monster on page 16.

THE PRINCESS AND THE MAGIC POTION

SCENE	PUPPETS		HANDS
1	KING	John	Peter
	DOCTOR	Michael	Jane
	PRINCESS	Mary	Anne
2	KING	John	John
	JOEY	Michael	
	PRINCESS	Mary	Anne
3	PRINCESS	Mary	Anne
	CATERPILLAR	Peter	John
4 & 5	PRINCESS	Mary	Anne
	CATERPILLAR	Peter	John
	GIANT	Michael	Jane
6	PRINCESS	Mary	Anne
	GIANT	Michael	Peter
	MONSTER	Jane	

Inventing Puppets

Inventing puppets is not difficult. Suppose you want to make the Doctor who examines the Princess, he could be a stick puppet. He could have a plastic bottle head and he could be going bald with just a few tufts of fur fabric glued to his scalp. You could dress him in a white coat and give him pipe cleaner glasses. Or you could make one of the animals into a Doctor. We have dressed up the wolf in a white coat and pipe cleaner glasses.

A Call Sheet

Real puppeteers write a call sheet and pin it up behind the stage to tell them who is going to work each puppet. This is a call sheet for this play. Make one yourself.

Grasping Things

As the Giant has human hands he is very good at grabbing. Make him tear things, squeeze things and pick smaller puppets up and examine them.

Giant's Voice

Don't forget about sound effects. Use the megaphone for the Giant's voice (page 29). You could have crashes of thunder every time he laughs too (page 32).

A Giant Sandwich

pieces of card

glue

Crumple a piece of green crêpe paper so that it looks like a lettuce leaf. Glue it inside two long pieces of thick card. Paint the card white or brown like this.

Dragon's Teeth

This is a story of a silly Dragon who steals a box of lollies and eats them all. His friends are jealous of him because he is in a toothpaste advertisement and they laugh when he gets toothache. Only a spider will help but he offers to pull out the Dragon's teeth. When the cat chases some mice, the Dragon decides to help them hide. Will they help him to cure his toothache in return? That is for you to decide. You will find the puppet Dragon on page 17, Little Girl on page 10, Spider and Mice on page 4, Cat and Wolf on page 20.

Scene 1

The Dragon's teeth are so nice that he's going to be in an advertisement for toothpaste. All the animals are very envious. The little girl gives him an ice lolly as a reward.

Cleaning Dragon's Teeth

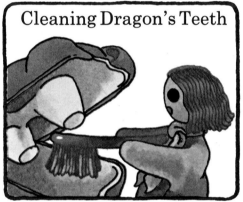

Clean the Dragon's teeth with a tooth brush. Hold it between your thumb and outer fingers and move your hand backwards and forwards.

Scene 2

The Dragon likes the lolly so much that he runs off with a whole box of them. The other animals follow him. He eats so many that he gets terrible toothache.

Eating Ice Lollies

Make a card ice lolly, hold it in the same way as the brush and put it into the Dragon's open mouth. Make the Dragon close his mouth. It looks as if he has eaten it.

Scene 3

He asks a Spider to help him. Spider gets a rope to pull the tooth out. 'I'll lose my job if I don't have any teeth,' says the Dragon. So the Spider goes off with his rope.

Scene 4

The Dragon asks the Wolf and Cat for help. The Wolf shakes his head and the Cat laughs. Then the Finger

Mice come on. The Cat sees them and chases them off the stage.

Pulling out Teeth

Make the Spider come on pulling a big heavy rope. Hold it between your two thumbs and pretend that it's very heavy to pull.

Scene 5

The Cat chases the Mice round and round. The Dragon watches. He decides to help the Mice. He

tells them that they can hide in his mouth and promises not to hurt them. They agree.

The Chase

Keep the Dragon in front with the Finger Mice. The other animals come on one behind the other, so they won't bump into each other during the chase.

Scene 6

When the Cat isn't looking the Mice climb into the Dragon's open mouth. The Dragon shuts his

mouth carefully. The Cat still runs round and round but he can't find the mice anywhere......
(*Finish the story your way.*)

Hiding the Mice

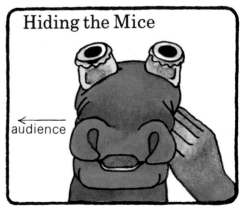

← audience

Open the Dragon's mouth. Put the Finger Mice in on the side that the audience can't see. Shut his mouth and the Finger Mice won't be seen.

Going Further

Reading about Puppets

If you have enjoyed this book, you may want to have a look at other books about puppets. Here are some to look out for.

Art of the Puppet	Bill Baird	(Plays, Inc. USA 1965)
Bandicoot and His Friends	Violet Philpott	(Dent 1970)
Bench Book (2) of Puppetry	H. W. Whanslaw	(Wells, Gardner 1948)
Caspar and his Friends	H. Baumann	(Dent 1965)
Dictionary of Puppetry	A. R. Philpott	(Macdonald 1969)
Eight Plays for Hand Puppets	A. R. Philpott	(Garnet Miller 1968)
Exploring Puppetry	Stuart and Pat Robinson	(Mills & Boon 1967)
Let's Look at Puppets	A. R. Philpott	(Muller 1966)
Modern Puppetry	A. R. Philpott	(Michael Joseph 1966)
Let's Make Puppets	A. R. Philpott	(Evans 1972)
Punch and Judy	P. Fraser	(Batsford)
Punch and Judy	G. Speaight	(Studio Vista 1970)
Puppet Circus	P. Fraser	(Batsford 1971)
St George and the Dragon	D. John	(Penguin 1963)
Your Puppetry	John Wright	(Sylvan Press 1951)

A bit about Glue

When you stick cloth to cloth, use Copydex. When you stick sponge to anything, use Bostik 1 or UHU. For gluing anything else use Bostik 1.

Puppet Workshops

You might write to one of the addresses on the opposite page to find out whether there is a puppet workshop near you.

Puppet Shows

If you want to become a really good puppeteer, go and watch as many puppet shows as you can find. Look for the tricks the professionals use and see if you can learn to do them yourself.

Puppet Collections

Several Museums around the world have collections of puppets. Your local museum will probably know where the best collections are.

Index

Finding out More

You should be able to find out more about puppets by writing to
any one of the following addresses:

Puppet Centre,
Battersea Town Hall,
Community Arts Centre,
Lavender Hill,
London, S.W.11.

Mrs. E. Murray,
UNIMA,
'Moonahwarra',
Lawson Road,
Springwood 2777,
Australia.

Puppetry Guild,
Mrs. Clarke,
28, Baal Street,
Palmyra 6157,
West Australia.

Lilian Herzberg,
19, Saldhausen Avenue,
Claremont,
Cape Town,
South Africa.